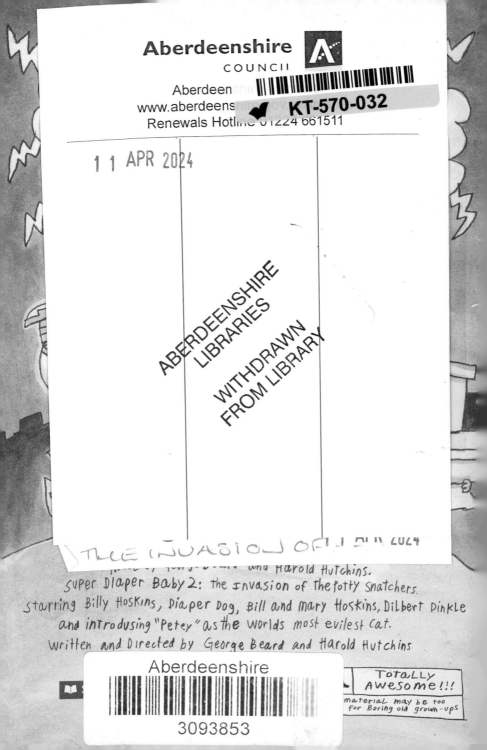

THE INVASION OF 1 APR 2024

...and Harold Hutchins.

Super Diaper Baby 2: the Invasion of the Potty Snatchers.
Starring Billy Hoskins, Diaper Dog, Bill and Mary Hoskins, Dilbert Dinkle
and introdusing "Petey" as the worlds most evilest cat.
Written and Directed by George Beard and Harold Hutchins

TOTALLY
AWESOME!!!

...material may be too
...for boring old grown-ups

For Madison
Mancini

SCHOLASTIC CHILDREN'S BOOKS
AN IMPRINT OF SCHOLASTIC LTD
EUSTON HOUSE, 24 EVERSHOLT STREET
LONDON, NW1 1DB, UK
REGISTERED OFFICE: WESTFIELD ROAD, SOUTHAM, WARWICKSHIRE, CV47 ORA
SCHOLASTIC AND ASSOCIATED LOGOS ARE TRADEMARKS AND/OR
REGISTERED TRADEMARKS OF SCHOLASTIC INC.

FIRST PUBLISHED IN THE US BY SCHOLASTIC INC, 2011
FIRST PUBLISHED IN THE UK BY SCHOLASTIC LTD, 2011
THIS EDITION PUBLISHED IN 2012

TEXT AND ILLUSTRATION COPYRIGHT © DAV PILKEY, 2011
COVER ILLUSTRATION COPYRIGHT © DAV PILKEY, 2011

THE RIGHT OF DAV PILKEY TO BE IDENTIFIED AS THE AUTHOR
AND ILLUSTRATOR OF THIS WORK HAS BEEN ASSERTED BY HIM.

ISBN 978 1407 13091 0

A CIP CATALOGUE RECORD FOR THIS BOOK IS AVAILABLE FROM THE BRITISH LIBRARY.

PRINTED IN THE UK BY CPI (UK) LTD, CROYDON, CRO 4YY.
PAPERS USED BY SCHOLASTIC CHILDREN'S BOOKS ARE MADE
FROM WOOD GROWN IN SUSTAINABLE FORESTS.

1 3 5 7 9 10 8 6 4 2

WWW.SCHOLASTIC.CO.UK/ZONE

It was the story of a baby who acksidently fell into some super power juice.

Splash

He drank it and got super powers and stuff.

Also, a dog drank the juice.

Glug

glug

He became super powery, too!

The baby and the dog are best friends now and they live together with their mum and dad.

They both wear diapers too!

Panel 1: one time a evil guy tried to Steal Super Diaper Babys Powers...

Transfer Helmet

This is going to be sweet!

Panel 2: ...but he made a boo-boo and got Turned into poo-poo!

Hey!

Transfer Helmet

Panel 3: Then he got some New clear waste on him and he grew way bigger and eviler!!!

Rar!

New clear Power Plant

Panel 4: So Super Diaper Baby and Diaper Dog Flew into action!

We'll get you Deputy Doo-Doo!

nuh-uh!!!

6

7

8

9

So George and Harold starded creating their all-new epic Novel, Super Diaper Baby 2.

I bet MR KRUPP will be super happy!

Me too!

They bet wrong.

What the---

This is even more offensiver than your Last Book !!!

So thats the story of how Super Diaper Baby 2 was invented.

DETENSHON

as usual, we hope you Like it more than Mr Krupp Did.

BIZZY WORK

BIZZY WORK

10

Chapters

Forwerd................. 3

1. A day at the Park ... 13

2. Meanwhile............. 37

3. Daddy DiLema...... 61

4 (Part 1). Meanwhile 2 ... 75

4 (Part 2). How the
   Pee Stoled Potties...... 85

5. The Aftermath........ 119

6. The Revenge of
   Rip Van Tinkle........ 151

7. Fathers Day 173

15

FLIP·O·RAMA

HEres How it works!!!!

STEP 1
Place your Left hand inside the dotted Lines marked "LeFt Hand Here". Hold The Book open FLAT.

STEP 2
GRasp the Right-hand Page with YOUR Right thumb and index finger (inside the dotted Lines marked Right Thumb Here").

STEP 3
Now Quickly FLip The Right-hand Page back and fourth until the Pitcher appears To Be Animated!

(for extra fun, try adding Your own sound Afecks).

17

FLIP-O-RAMA #1

(pages **19** and **21**)

Remember, Flip <u>only</u> page 19.
While you are Flipping, be
shure you can see the
Pitcher on page 19 <u>And</u> the
one on page 21.

IF you Flip Quickly,
The two pitchers will
start to look like
<u>one</u>   Animated Pitcher.

Dont forget to
add your own
Sound Afecks!

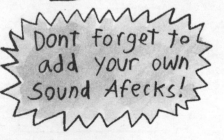

Left Hand
Here

Down Goes the Airplane...

Right
thumb
Here

Up Goes the Airplane...

Down go the airplane

23

Right Thumb Here

up go the airplane

26

29

30

32

34

36

38

40

42

43

44

45

46

47

49

50

Panel 1: Hey, what about me? I still need WATER!

Panel 2: I don't see **YOU** payin' NO bills!

SO ANYWAYS...

Panel 3: 2 weeks later... I'm Home! you didnt pay our water bill, did you?

52

53

FLIP-O-RAMA 3

If you forgot how to do this already, please see your doctor. Afterwards, Turn to page 17 for further instruckshons.

Left Hand Here.

Drinking Dr Dinkle

55

Drinking Dr Dinkle

58

59

60

Snatcher Catchers

63

Right
Thumb
Here

Snatcher catchers

Jacker Smackers

67

Right Thumb Here

Jacker Smackers

Cheater Beaters!

Right thumb Here

Cheater Beaters!

74

76

77

80

81

82

83

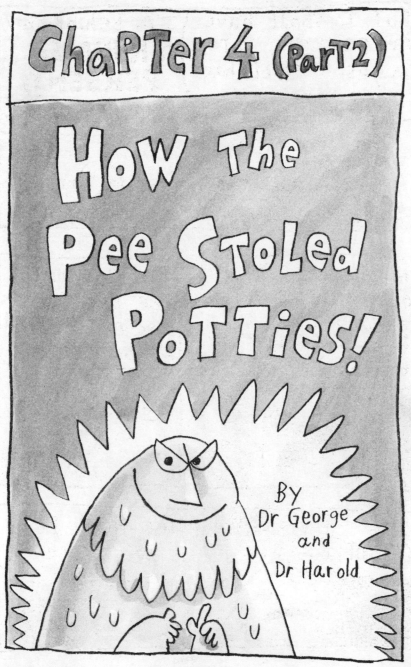

That Night Rip Van Tinkle
was frowning a frown,
as he sneered at the houses
below in the town.

No one Knows why he was
feeling so ruthless...
It could be because all his
money was useless.

Or maybe because he was
just feeling cranky.
Or possibly cuz his bad breath
was so stanky.
But we think the very best
reason might be
that he smelled like a bucket
of twelve-day-old pee.

But whatever the reason
    his stank or his dough,
he stood up there hating
    the people below.
He snarled as he frowned
    feeling drearier and drearier.
"Those Jerks in the city
Think Theyr'e so superier!

"They all be hatin'!
   But heres what I think:
I think things would change
   if they started to stink!

If all of those idiots
   smelled just like pee,
they wouldent be goin' Round
disrespectin' me!!!"

89

And then Rip Van Tinkle
Thought up a idea.
But we couldent Think up
a rhyme for "idea".

"I Know just what to do"
he started professin'.
"I'LL teach all of those good-
smelling people a Lessen!"

91

So he took some scrap metal
and used an old wheel
to build a contrapshon
with teeth made of steel.

He hammered its tail
and sharpened its claws,
and welded its wiskers
and titened its Jaws.

It took 24 hours
    From when he'd begun,
'Till the Robo-Kitty
    Three Thousand was done.
"ALL I need is a driver.
    I need someone mean.
I need someone evil ❤
    to run my machine".

So he took his cat "Petey"
    and strapped him in tight...

...Then both of those villens sneaked out in the night.

"Watch this," Rip Van Tinkle said
Laffing out Loud...
and soon he began to
turn into a cloud.

And when the pee cloud
was over the town,
the thunderclaps crashed
and the pee drops rained down.

Into the chimneys
the pee drops they flew
And they entered each house
knowing just what to do.

Each drop found a wrench...

... and each wrench found a bolt...

JOLT

...and soon every toilet popped up with a JOLT!

They carried each toilet
Right out of each house, and
Into the jaws of the
Kitty Three thousend.

crunch! crunch! went the robot
without too much trouble
and soon every potty
was crushed into rubbel!

But in one little house,
on one little street,
One drip heard the sounds
of two little feet.

The pee drop looked up
and what did it see?
but a cute little tot
with a fluffy blankie.

The baby looked down
and said, "MR Pee, Hey!
Why are you taking
our toilet away?"

And that mean little drip,
do you know what it did?
Why, it made up a lie
and it said to the kid:

"Your toilet is broken---
it squeaks when you flush it.
I'll take it away and I'll
clean it and brush it.

I'll shine it right up
 --I'll fix it and oil it,
and soon I'll return with a
Good-as-new toilet."

And the baby believed what
the pee drop had said.
So it got him a juice box
and took him to bed.

And at last when the baby
was sleeping and dreaming,
that nasty old pee drop
went on with its skeeming!

He carried the Toilet
Right out the door.
And once it was crushed,
He went back to get more.

The snatching of Potties
went on through the night,
And into the dawn of the
Mornings first Light.

And Once Every toilet
was crushed by the cat,
The people awoke and cried,
"What up wit' dat?"

"Our toilets are gone!
We've got to go potty!
Oh, we do not like this!
Oh, no we do notty!"

So they each crossed their legs
and squirmed all around,
And they squeezed and they clenched,
and they bobbed up and down.

'Till all of the people
were doing "Pee dances"
Shouting, "Someone please help us,
or we'll wet our pantses!"

113

They wiggled all morning
    in torment and Trauma,
Just Like they're doing
    in this Flip-o-Rama →

Left Hand
Here

Pee-Dance
RevoLushon

Right
Thumb
Here

Pee-Dance
RevoLushon

Soon, warm liquid streams
with yellowish Hues
Flowed down their legs
and filled up their shoes.

And they sobbed as they stood
in their puddles of piddle,
But no one could help them.
Not even a Little.

CHAPTER 5

the Aftermath

121

124

125

126

127

129

130

131

132

133

134

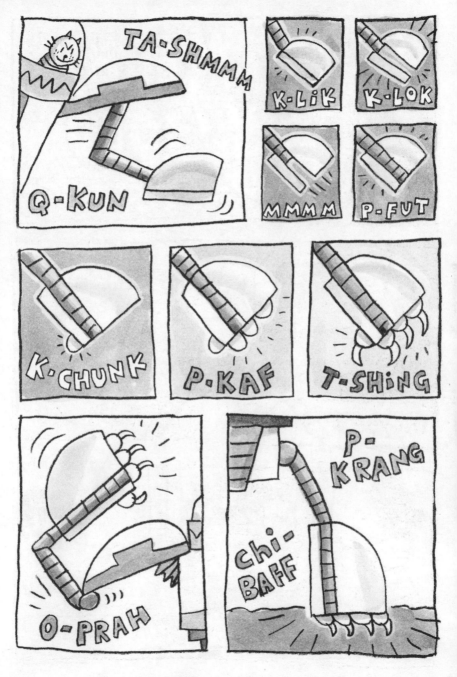

136

138

139

140

141

Koo-Koo For Kitty Nip!

Right
thumb
Here

Koo-Koo For Kitty Nip!

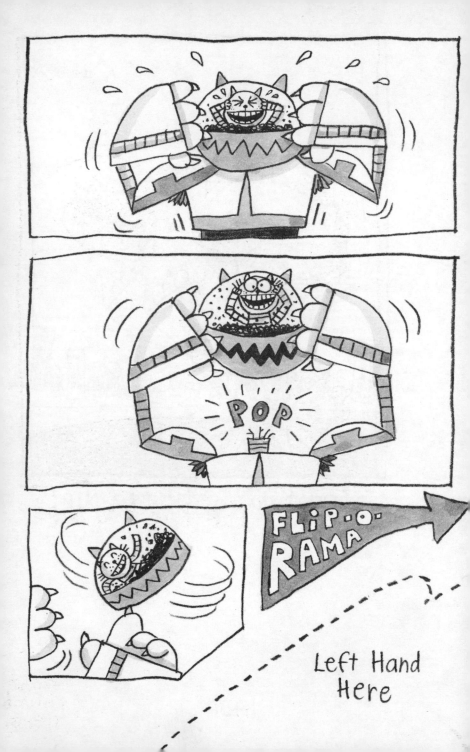

POP

FLIP·O·RAMA

Left Hand
Here

KITTY FOR KOO-KOO NIP!

147

KiTTY FOR KOO-KOO NiP!

150

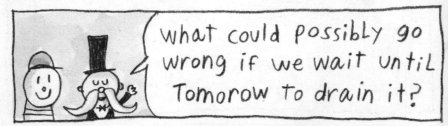

154

156

160

161

FLiP·O·RAMA

Left Hand Here

Building Basher

Right thumb Here

Building Basher

166

169

170

Chapter 7

"Fathers Day"

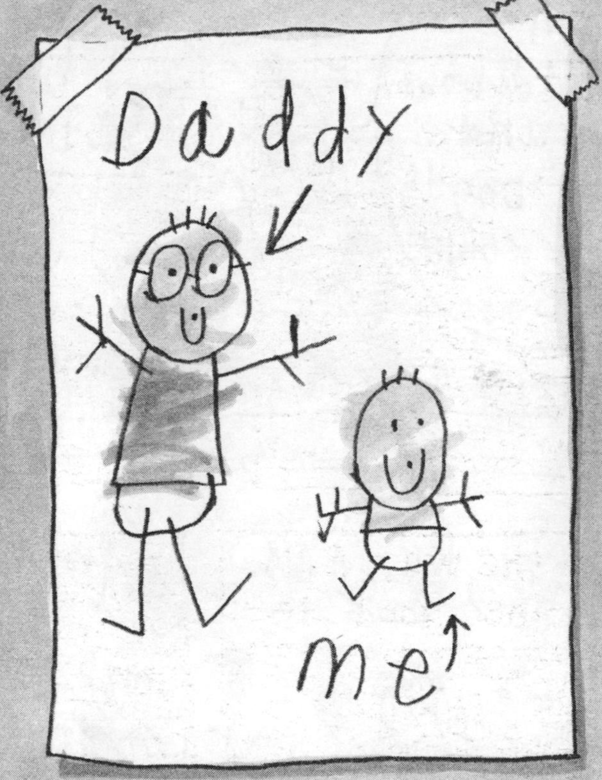

Hi mummy and Daddy!
BILLY!
Daddy Theres a big Ice monster outside!!!
Im so glad your safe!!!
Daddy Look at the ice monster!!
OK, OK. LeTs Look at this silly ice monster of yours!
ILL JusT open these curTins and take a peek!

AND SO

I'm a Big, evil ice monster...

...And I'm gonna destroy the WorLd!!!

Umm... Well, I wish you wouldent do that.
why not???
Because, um... its not very nice.
Well what are you Gonna do about it, huh?
Umm... Umm...
me shure is proud of you, daddy! your super brave!!!
really?

If you destroy the world, I might get mad!!!
Oh No! NOT That!!!
PULL
PULL
How come hes shaking Like that???
me think hes ascared of you, daddy!

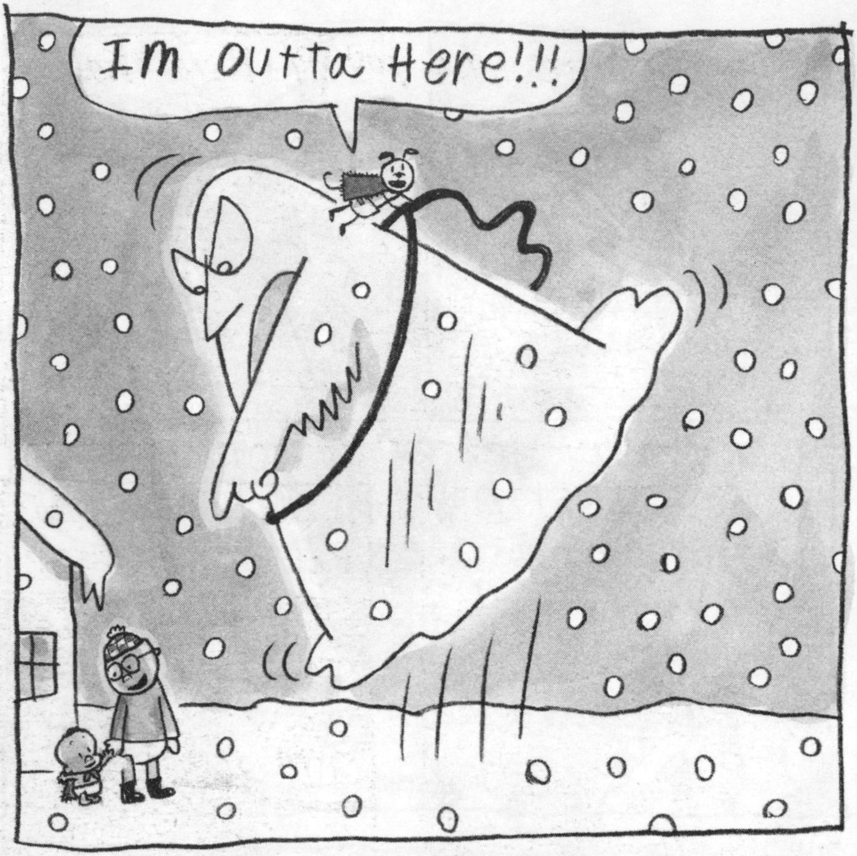
Im outta Here!!!

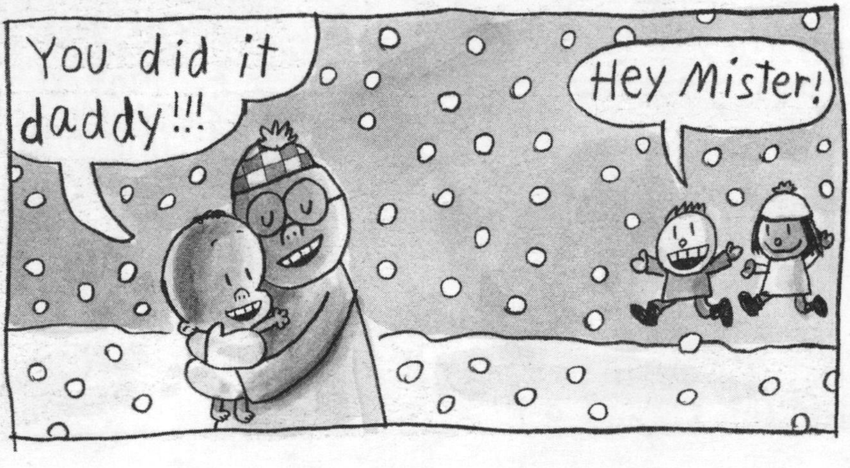
You did it daddy!!!
Hey Mister!

183

Then Billy and Diaper Dog moved the Earth back to its proper place in space...
zip
...and flew back home to Join the Celebrashon!
Hey it stopped snowing!
Can I take a pitcher of the Hero Dad for our newspaper?
OK
Hooray!!!
Left Hand Here.

say Cheese!!!

Right
thumb
Here

say Cheese!!!

READ GEORGE AND HAROLD'S
FIRST TWO EPIC ADVENTURES!

Faster than a speeding stroller, more powerful than diaper rash, and able to leap tall buildings without making poopy-stinkers, it's Super Diaper Baby!

Meet Ook and Gluk, the two coolest caveboys to step out of the Stone Age!

CAPTAIN UNDERPANTS
AND THE TERRIFYING RE-TURN OF TIPPY TINKLETROUSERS

Whatever happened to Professor Poopypants, that tiny tornado of terror who traumatized the people of Piqua? He changed his name to Tippy Tinkletrousers, and he has a special surprise for anybody who thinks his NEW name is still funny. This looks like another job for the amazing Captain Underpants!